The Tiara Club

Also in the Tiara Club

VIVIAN FRENCH

The Tiara Club

Princess Katie
AND THE
Silver Pony

ILLUSTRATED BY SARAH GIBB

KATHERINE TEGEN BOOKS
An Imprint of HarperCollins*Publishers*

The Tiara Club: Princess Katie and the Silver Pony
Text copyright © 2007 by Vivian French
Illustrations copyright © 2007 by Sarah Gibb

Library of Congress Cataloging-in-Publication Data
French, Vivian.
Princess Katie and the silver pony / Vivian French ; illustrated
by Sarah Gibb. — 1st U.S. ed.
p.   cm. — (The Tiara Club)
Summary: Princess Katie and the other princesses at the
Princess Academy must make one carefully chosen wish in order
to win a chance to be in the Royal Parade.
ISBN-10: 0-06-112432-X (trade bdg.)
ISBN-13: 978-0-06-112432-7 (trade bdg.)
ISBN-10: 0-06-112430-3 (pbk.)
ISBN-13: 978-0-06-112430-3 (pbk.)
[1. Princesses—Fiction. 2. Wishes—Fiction. 3. Parades—
Fiction. 4. Magic—Fiction. 5. Schools—Fiction.]   I. Gibb,
Sarah, ill. II. Title.
PZ7.F88917Prnk 2007   2006019224
[Fic]—dc22   CIP
                                                    AC

Typography by Amy Ryan

❖

First U.S. edition, 2007

*For Princess Lisa,
with lots of love
x*
—V.F.

*For four little princes: Alex, Finlay,
Xavier, and Felix*
—S.G.

The Royal Palace Academy
for the Preparation of Perfect Princesses
(Known to our students as "The Princess Academy")

OUR SCHOOL MOTTO:
*A Perfect Princess always thinks of others before herself,
and is kind, caring, and truthful.*

We offer the complete curriculum for all princesses, including:

How to Talk to a Dragon

Creative Cooking for Perfect Palace Parties

Wishes, and How to Use Them Wisely

Designing and Creating the Perfect Ball Gown

Avoiding Magical Mistakes

Descending a Staircase as if Floating on Air

Our principal, Queen Gloriana, is present at all times, and students are in the excellent care of the school Fairy Godmother.

VISITING TUTORS AND EXPERTS INCLUDE:

KING PERCIVAL *(Dragons)*

LADY VICTORIA *(Banquets)*

QUEEN MOTHER MATILDA *(Etiquette, Posture, and Poise)*

THE GRAND HIGH DUCHESS DELIA *(Fashion)*

We award tiara points to encourage
our princesses toward the next level.
Each princess who earns enough points
in her first year is welcomed to the
Tiara Club and presented with a silver tiara.

Tiara Club princesses are invited to return
next year to Silver Towers, our very special
residence for Perfect Princesses, where they
may continue their education at a higher level.

PLEASE NOTE:
Princesses are expected to arrive
at the Academy with a *minimum* of:

TWENTY BALL GOWNS
*(with all necessary hoops,
petticoats, etc.)*

TWELVE DAY-DRESSES

SEVEN GOWNS
*suitable for garden parties
and other special daytime
occasions*

TWELVE TIARAS

DANCING SHOES
five pairs

VELVET SLIPPERS
three pairs

RIDING BOOTS
two pairs

*Cloaks, muffs, stoles, gloves,
and other essential
accessories, as required*

How do you do? It's great to meet you . . . we're all so glad you're here! Oh! Maybe you don't know who we are. We're the Princesses Katie (that's me), Charlotte, Emily, Alice, Daisy, and Sophia, and we share the Rose Room at the Princess Academy, and one day we'll all be members of the totally fabulous Tiara Club! Just as long as we get enough tiara points, of course.

Do you ever feel really tired after a party? Well, we had a wonderful Birthday Ball here at the Academy, but for the next few days it was so hard to get up. . . .

Chapter One

I couldn't believe it. The alarm clock was ringing and ringing! I put my pillow over my head and shut my eyes tightly.

Whoomph! The pillow was snatched away, and there was Princess Alice smiling at me.

"Give up," she said cheerfully. "Fairy G.'s been in twice already, and if we don't get down to breakfast in ten minutes, we'll *all* get minus tiara points and *none* of us will ever be members of the Tiara Club!"

"I'm tired!" I moaned.

"Cheer up!" Princess Sophia plonked herself down on my bed. "It's Friday today, so tomorrow's Saturday—"

"And that's the day of the Royal Parade!" Charlotte and Emily shouted together. Daisy threw her pillow in the air.

"And we'll all be wearing our

very best dresses!" she crowed.

I groaned and crawled out of bed.

"Eight minutes!" Alice warned me. "Please hurry up, Katie—we simply *can't* have our Rose Room beaten by Princess Perfecta and her creepy crew."

That did make me hurry. In fact, I totally zoomed into my clothes. Princess Perfecta always likes to be best at everything, and she's such a show-off. She was here last year, so she should be a senior—and a member of the Tiara Club, but she didn't get enough tiara points! So

she's back in Year One with us, and that's made her as mean as a snake—at least, that's what Alice's big sister says.

As soon as I was dressed, we rushed out of the dormitory and down the winding staircase. We were halfway down when Alice

stopped so suddenly we almost fell on top of her.

"Look!" she gasped, and she pointed out of the tower window.

We looked and we gasped too.

The most beautiful coach any of us had ever seen was parked by the front steps of the Academy. It was

shaped like a wonderful pearly seashell, and it was sparkling all over in the sunshine. The seats were covered in softly gleaming white satin cushions, and snow-white furry rugs were heaped everywhere. Six ponies, harnessed with silver bridles and silver reins, were in between the shafts, and tiny silver bells tinkled every time they shook their heads.

"It's magic!" I whispered. We gazed at it in absolute rapture until Sophia said, "Oh, no! Look at the time!"

We made it to breakfast just in time. The dining hall is very long, with portraits of amazingly grand and gracious princesses all along the walls. Our teachers sit at the far end on golden thrones, but we sit on benches at wooden tables, and we actually eat on china plates!

Sophia was *so* shocked when she first arrived (she had never eaten

off anything except gold plates), but Charlotte pointed out the food would taste the same, so Sophia didn't make a big deal about it.

Because we were so late, we had to sit at the end of the table—and there were Perfecta and Floreen.

"Oh, goodness me." Perfecta

sneered, looking at Emily and Daisy's bird's-nest hair. "I can see what kind of wish *you'll* be making this morning. *You'll* be wishing for a hairbrush!" And she and Floreen laughed as if she'd made the best joke ever.

"Ignore her!" Sophia hissed under her breath, but Emily was looking at Perfecta with wide eyes.

"What do you mean?" she asked. "What wish?"

"What?" Perfecta threw up her hands as if Emily had asked her

something really stupid.

"You mean . . . you don't *know*?" She sniggered loudly. "It's Wish Class this morning." She turned to Floreen as they got up from the table. "Don't you think it's *quite* extraordinary that Queen Gloriana lets such dumb princesses into the Academy?"

Chapter Two

katie

*J*ust as I was finishing my breakfast, Queen Gloriana came sailing into the dining hall. She's our principal, and she's wonderfully tall and graceful. She's also a little bit scary, because she expects us to be *perfect* Princesses—and sometimes that can be very hard work. I was pleased to see Fairy G. stomping in behind her. Fairy G. is much more fun. She's the school's Fairy Godmother, and she keeps an eye on all of us.

"Good morning, my dear young princesses," Queen Gloriana said, and paused while we made our curtsies.

I didn't do too badly, but Charlotte wobbled a lot and clutched at the table. A butter dish crashed onto the floor, and of course *everybody* turned and stared. Charlotte blushed bright red, and Perfecta and Floreen sniggered.

Queen Gloriana went on speaking as if nothing had happened. "As you know, princesses, tomorrow is the Royal Parade, and this year there will be something a little special. Our good friend King Constantin of Forever and Faraway has been kind enough to give the school a very beautiful coach. I have decided that the princess who has the most tiara points by the end of the day will ride in the Seashell Coach and lead the Parade!"

Immediately there was a burst of whispering. *Imagine riding in that gorgeous coach!*

Tap, tap! Fairy G. tapped a chair.

"Time for everyone to go to Wish Class! Follow me!"

"Wow!" Alice whispered in my

ear. "Do you think we can wish for anything we want?" Her eyes were dancing, and I began to feel excited as I followed Sophia and Emily out into the long black-and-white marble corridor that led to the classrooms. Daisy and Charlotte

were right behind, and so were
Perfecta and Floreen.

"I know *someone* who needs to
wish she can curtsey properly,"
Floreen said spitefully as we
hurried after Fairy G.

The classroom wasn't very fancy,

except for a beautiful sparkly chandelier that glittered in the light. The four tables were just plain wood, and the chairs weren't covered in satin or anything like that—although they did have soft, red velvet cushions. Charlotte, Sophia, Emily, Daisy, Alice, and I managed to get a table to ourselves.

I couldn't help smiling when I saw the other princesses trying to avoid having Perfecta and Floreen sit with them.

"Now, listen carefully!" Fairy G. boomed at us. She's very big, and her voice is really loud. "You will each have one wish, and one wish only. Think hard, and then write it down. Remember, once it's written down, it can't be changed."

She fished in her pocket, brought out a huge alarm clock, and banged it down on her desk.

"You have five minutes! *Begin!*"

At once we could hear murmurings from the other tables.

Princess Freya called out, "Please, Fairy G., are we meant to be thinking of something princessy? Or can we wish for whatever we want?"

Fairy G. smiled a mysterious sort of smile. "That's for me to know, and you to find out," she said.

"Oh." Freya looked confused.

"So can I wish for a kitten?"

Fairy G. didn't answer.

Princess Perfecta snorted loudly. *"Really!"* she said. "Imagine wanting a *kitten!*"

"That's right," Floreen agreed. "Some princesses are *so* babyish."

"I don't see anything wrong with wanting a kitten," I said loudly.

"I'd like . . ." My mind whirled, and I thought of the Seashell Coach. "A pony!"

I had an idea. The ponies pulling the Seashell Coach had been pretty, but somehow not quite right—and I knew what would be *exactly* perfect!

"A *silver* pony!"

"Ooooh!" Beside me, Emily's eyes lit up.

"That's fantastic, Katie!" said Charlotte.

"Wouldn't it be so cute?" Sophia and Daisy sighed.

"Just imagine!" Alice said. "A

silver pony. We could feed it lumps of sugar . . ."

"Well," I said slowly, "I was more thinking of—"

"Time's up!" boomed Fairy G. "I'm coming around to collect your wishes now."

We looked at each other.

"So should we?" Charlotte whispered. "Should we all wish for silver ponies? One each?"

"Yes!" I said, much too loudly. I saw Perfecta glare at me. "Six silver ponies—to pull the Seashell Coach. They'd be fabulous!"

And we all scribbled quickly as Fairy G. stomped up to our table to collect our wishes.

Chapter Three

Nothing happened. There was no sign of any magic. Fairy G. went back to her desk and sorted through the pieces of paper.

"Hmm," she said. "Very creative. And now for your tiara points."

We all sat up straight in our

seats. *Tiara points?*

"That's right." Fairy G. gave us an odd kind of smile. "Queen Gloriana has asked me to give one hundred tiara points to the princess who has asked for the most

thoughtful and unselfish wish."

I could feel my eyes popping out of my head. *One hundred points!* That would mean—

"Exactly!" Fairy G. knew what I was thinking—and every other princess in the class. "One hundred points will earn you a place in the Seashell Coach!"

"But that's not fair!" Princess Eglantine's face was bright red. She was a friend of Perfecta's—at least, she was when Perfecta allowed her to be. "That's *so* not fair! I'd *never* have wished for curly blonde hair if I'd known that!"

Have I told you that Fairy G. is

big? Well, when Eglantine said that, the Fairy Godmother grew *enormous*!

She looked so scary, I would have dived under the table if I hadn't been too frightened to move.

"Princess Eglantine," Fairy G. roared, "you will take twenty *minus* tiara points! *No* princess worthy of the name should ever speak the way you have just spoken."

Eglantine cowered in her seat, and whispered, "Sorry, Fairy G."

"*Harrrumph!*" Fairy G. still looked angry, but she shrank back to her usual size. "Let me remind you all that a Perfect Princess should never *ever* need to be told to think of others before herself."

I began to feel nervous. *What would Fairy G. think about our silver ponies? Would she give us minus tiara points too?*

"Now," Fairy G. said firmly, "it's time to announce the winner. Are you ready?"

We sat up, folded our hands in our laps, and nodded. I could feel my heart pitter-pattering in my chest, even though I knew I couldn't possibly win.

"And the winner is—" Fairy G. stopped for a dramatic pause.

We all held our breath.

"And the winner is—Princess Perfecta!"

There was a long silence. I could see Perfecta smiling a very self-satisfied smile.

"Princess Perfecta, please read your winning wish out to the class," Fairy G. said, handing Perfecta back her piece of paper.

Perfecta stood up.

"I wish, not for a perfect face, but truthful heart and perfect grace," she said in a singsong voice.

Beside me, Alice gasped loudly.

"What is it?" I whispered.

"She's a cheat!" she hissed.

"Silence!" boomed Fairy G., but then she did something very odd. She gave Alice a sly little wink.

"And now, class dismissed! Your wishes will be waiting for you in the Great Hall," Fairy G. went on. She smiled a huge smile at Perfecta. "And I'm sure we *all* wish you well, Princess Perfecta—enjoy your wish and your ride in the Seashell Coach."

We scrambled out of the classroom. We tried hard to walk calmly down the long corridor that led to the Great Hall, but at the same time we were dying to get there as fast as we could.

Would there really be six silver ponies waiting for us? I couldn't wait!

As we scooted along, Alice was almost exploding with rage. "Perfecta cheated!" she said. "That was my sister's wish last year! Why on earth didn't Fairy G. say something?"

I was remembering Fairy G.'s little wink. "I think Fairy G. is up to something," I said, and then we were at the door of the Great Hall.

It was *amazing*.

Princess Katie

Go to *www.tiaraclubbooks.com!*
Enter the secret word from each book. Download dazzling
posters you can decorate with your Tiara Club stickers.

KATHERINE TEGEN BOOKS • *An Imprint of* HarperCollins*Publishers* • Sticker art © 2007 by PiA?

Chapter Four

You know when it's a sunny day, and little golden sparkles of dust float in the sunbeams? Well, the Great Hall was full of sparkles just like that, only much much sparklier. Most of our class was already there, and we could see princesses spinning around and around in fantastic ball gowns, or dancing like ballerinas.

Lisa and Jemima were singing like nightingales. Nancy was walking up and down on stilts. Freya was stroking a fluffy kitten. It was incredible! And up at the far

end of the room Queen Gloriana was talking to Fairy G. and some of the other teachers.

Eglantine, Floreen, and Perfecta were in front of us. As each of them walked through the door, they *changed*! Eglantine suddenly had tons and tons of long golden curls, and as Floreen pushed her out of the way, I could see her eyes shining.

Then Floreen was in amongst the sparkles, and *oooomph*! She was wearing the highest high-heeled shoes ever, and they were covered with glittering jewels, and she wasn't wobbling even the tiniest bit as she walked.

Perfecta was next. She turned to look at us just before she walked in, and she said in her nastiest voice, "Oh, it's the Rose Roomers! If you're *very* lucky, I might wave to

you from the Seashell Coach!"

Then she walked into the Great Hall—but nothing seemed to happen, except she made a funny kind of *"oh!"* sound and sat down hard on the floor.

Alice, Charlotte, Sophia, Emily, Daisy, and I were too excited to take much notice. We each took a deep breath and ran into the Great Hall together.

Ooooooh!

Six fabulous silver ponies were trotting around and around the hall, shaking their silver manes and tails and whinnying loudly.

They were so beautiful—but

then Floreen gave a massive screech,
and Lisa screamed. The ponies
flung up their heads and began to
gallop.

"Quick!" I said. "They're scared, poor ponies! We've got to catch them!"

This was easier said than done.

Now I know, and I'm sure you do too, that the very worst way to try and catch a pony is to run around making lots of noise. We know it—but it looked as if absolutely none of my classmates did. Freya whistled at them, Floreen went on screeching, Jemima tried to rush them into a corner— and then Nancy fell off her stilts with a dreadful clatter that sent those poor ponies into a perfect frenzy. They began to gallop this way and that, looking for a way out. But do you know what? Even though they were awfully scared, they were really careful not to crash

into anyone. They swerved this way and that, and sometimes they pirouetted on their silver hooves, and their manes and tails streamed behind them . . .

"Stop this at once!"

Queen Gloriana was furious!

Everyone froze—even the ponies. The whole Great Hall was as still and silent as if we'd all been turned to stone.

"*Who* is responsible for this *ridiculous* state of affairs?" Our principal's voice was as cold as ice, and I felt terrible. I just wished and wished the floor would open up and swallow me, but I also knew I had to confess. My knees were like jelly as I croaked, "It was me, Your Majesty."

"Princess Katie, I am *deeply* disappointed in you," Queen Gloriana snapped, and her eyes were positively flashing. I hung my head. "This is the most shocking—"

But she was interrupted.

Princess Perfecta walked calmly up to our principal, sank into a deep curtsey, and spoke in a grown-up voice we'd never ever heard her use before.

"If you please, Your Majesty, the fault was not intentional. Our

beloved Princess Katie meant no harm. Her wish was for the good of the school, and if Your Majesty will be gracious enough to permit me, I will explain."

Chapter Five

I don't think I've ever been so surprised in my entire life.

Alice grabbed my arm. "It's her wish," she said, and her eyes were sparkling. "It's come true!"

Perfecta went on, still in that strange, grown-up voice. "Your

Majesty must understand that we were each granted one wish. Princess Katie, having seen the wondrous beauty of the Seashell Coach, was concerned that the original ponies were not, perhaps, the most perfect match for such a grand carriage. With this thought in mind, and in true hopes of doing a good deed, Princess Katie put her own desires to one side and persuaded her dear friends to follow her noble example . . . and the result, as you can see, is six delightful silver ponies."

There was a stunned silence, and then everyone began to talk at once. Queen Gloriana held up her hand.

"Thank you, Princess Perfecta," she said. "I accept your explanation. Princess Katie! You and your friends may take your ponies to the royal stable, and . . ." She actually smiled! "You may care for them until the

Royal Parade tomorrow. The Seashell Coach will be, indeed, quite perfect."

I made my best curtsey ever. "Thank you very much, Your Majesty," I said. We were just

starting to move toward the ponies (they were standing quite still, as good as gold), when Perfecta made a very strange noise. It was a kind of strangled squeak, as if she was trying to stop herself from saying something, but absolutely *had* to say it. "Your Majesty," she said, or rather, kind of gurgled. "I have one more thing that must be said, for I have a truthful heart."

She gulped hard. "Your Majesty, and my fellow princesses, I have to confess to a terrible deed. I knew the importance of our wishes, and I . . ." She turned purple and truly looked as if she was choking on every word. "I stole my wish from the student who won last year. I am in no way worthy of one hundred tiara points, nor to take my position in the Seashell Coach. I humbly suggest, Your Most Royal Highness, that Princess Katie and her friends take my place."

"Well said, Princess Perfecta," Queen Gloriana said quietly. "It shall be so."

And then Perfecta burst into a flood of tears and rushed out of the Great Hall.

We were allowed to care for our ponies that whole afternoon and evening. After all the excitement, we were excused from lessons. Fairy G. said she had to do some private magic on the wooden floor of the Great Hall, because six feisty little ponies had made a terrible mess, but she didn't sound mad.

She also asked us if we knew that the wishes only lasted for twenty-four hours.

"Oh, no!" I said. "Does that mean the silver ponies disappear before the parade?"

Fairy G. chuckled. "We might manage an extension," she said. "Just this once. Queen Gloriana thinks you're right, Katie. The

Seashell Coach will look splendid! But they'll have to go after that."

She saw our unhappy faces and shook her head. "Cheer up! You've each got one hundred tiara points. And think about those other poor little ponies, not allowed to take part in the parade. They'll be longing for someone to give them a pat and a piece of apple!"

That made us feel bad. We hurried down to the stables. They were so cute . . . and, if I'm absolutely truthful, they were even nicer than our silver ponies because they were so real. Each of the silver ponies looked exactly the same, so

we could never tell which one was
which.

But they did look beautiful the

next day, when they came trotting up to get us for the Royal Parade, and we all stepped into the Seashell Coach.

Chapter Six

So what was the Royal Parade like?

It was perfect.

Princess Perfecta was still being truthful of heart and full of grace, and she insisted on doing our hair. She was amazing! She even managed to make my hair look more princessy. She put it up with some little glittery star clips of her own, and it looked wonderful! And then she wished us luck . . . and you'll never guess what happened next. I found myself actually feeling sorry for her—me, feeling sorry

for Princess Perfecta!

So I asked her if she'd like to ride in the Seashell Coach with us. She gave me a gracious smile and said in her funny grown-up voice, "You are a true princess, Princess Katie, but I must decline your most generous offer."

So Alice, Emily, Charlotte, Sophia, Daisy, and I sat on the white satin cushions with snow-white fur rugs over our knees and rolled away in the Seashell Coach.

Down the driveway we went, and away to the town. There were thousands of people cheering and waving at us.

So we smiled and waved back, and smiled some more until our faces were aching. When we got back to the Princess Academy, we were really tired.

"*Phew!*" Alice said, as we stepped carefully out of the Seashell Coach, trying hard not to step on the hems of our dresses. "That was *fun!*"

And then—

Ooomph!

The six silver ponies vanished.

So what did we do?

We changed out of our silk and satin and velvet gowns, and then we ran down to the stables to tell those cute little ponies all about the parade.

And as the smallest pony

snuffled her soft whiskery nose into the palm of my hand, hunting for more apple, I felt like the luckiest princess in the whole wide world. I had a hundred extra tiara points, a pony to pet, and—best of all—six of the very best friends a princess could have. Sophia, Charlotte, Daisy, Emily, Alice— and *you*!

What happens next?

FIND OUT IN

✦ *Princess Daisy* ✦
∽ AND THE ∽
Dazzling Dragon

Hello! And I really want to say hello to you the right way. Should I say, "Good day, Your Highness"? That doesn't sound very friendly, and I do want us to be friends! After all we're at the Princess Academy together, aren't we? Ooops! I nearly forgot to tell you—I'm Daisy! Princess Daisy. Have you met my other friends—Charlotte, Katie, Alice, Emily, and Sophia? They're learning to be Perfect Princesses, just like you and me. It's fun most of the time but Princess Perfecta isn't very nice. We're really really happy that she doesn't share the Rose Room dormitory with us. She's much too mean!

You are cordially invited to visit www.tiaraclubbooks.com!

Visit your special princess friends at their dazzling website!

Find the secret word hidden in each of the first six Tiara Club books. Then go to the Tiara Club website, enter the secret word, and get an exclusive poster. Print out the poster for each book and save it. When you have all six, put them together to make one amazing poster of the entire Royal Princess Academy. Use the stickers in the books to decorate and make your very own perfect princess academy poster.

More fun at www.tiaraclubbooks.com:

- Download your own Tiara Club membership card!

- Win future Tiara Club books.

- Get activities and coloring sheets with every new book.

- Stay up-to-date with the princesses in this great series!

Visit www.tiaraclubbooks.com and be a part of the Tiara Club!